Some of my good reviews:

'Will make you laugh out loud, cringe and snigger, all at the same time'
–LoveReading4Kids

'Very funny and cheeky'
–Booktictac, Guardian Online Review

Waterstones Children's Book Prize Shortlistee!

'WHAT'S NOT TO LOVE?'
–Sun

'I LAUGHED SO MUCH, I THOUGHT THAT I WAS GOING TO BURST!'
Finbar, aged 9

'The review of the eight year old boy in our house...
"Can I keep it to give to a friend?"
Best recommendation you can get' –Observer

'HUGELY ENJOYABLE. SURREAL CHAO...
–Guard...

I am still not a Loser
The Roald Dahl FUNNY PRIZE ...ER 2013

EGMONT

We bring stories to life

First published in Great Britain 2017
by Egmont UK Ltd, The Yellow Building,
1 Nicholas Road, London W11 4AN

Text and illustration copyright © Jim Smith 2017
The moral rights of Jim Smith have been asserted.

ISBN 978 1 4052 8721 0

barryloser.com
www.egmont.co.uk

A CIP catalogue record for this title is available from the British
Library

Printed and bound in Great Britain by the CPI Group

67256/003

Egmont takes its responsibility to the planet and its inhabitants
very seriously. We aim to use papers from well-managed forests
run by responsible suppliers.

Thanks to Liz Bankes for all her amazekeel help with this book!

Barry Loser's Christmas joke book!

Really badly wrapped up by

Jim Smith

Merry Keelmas!

Welcome to my amazekeel Christmas joke book! It's full of hilarikeel jokes, all of them written down by ME!

present from my granny

Comperleeterly
blank page.

Contents

Family funnies

Every Christmas, my whole family (and my best friend Bunky, because he's ALWAYS round my house), tell each other COMPERLEETERLY RUBBISH jokes.
I thought I'd write a few of them down so you could feel like one of the Losers too!

Why am I the keelest dad at Christmas?

Erm, dunno

Cos I'm a gangsta wrapper!

3

4

Reindeer jokes

You know how Santa's got loads of reindeer? Well here are some keeeel jokes about them.

ooh, looks like rain, dear

Which one out of Santa's eight billion reindeer has got no eyes?
No idea

Which one out of Santa's eight million reindeer has got no eyes and likes pretending to be asleep?

Still no idea.

he's <u>still</u> because he's asleep!

ZZZ

What one out of Santa's seven trillion reindeer has got a laptop on its head?

Umm...

Mac!

what, like a Mac computer?

Yeah!

But is 'Mac' a person's name?

Just go with it

10

Which one of Santa's reindeer lies outside Santa's door so people can wipe their shoes on him?

Matt!

He sounds like a stupid reindeer, doesn't he.

12

Do you know about the French reindeer who wears sandals? He's called

Philippe Flop!

but how does he fit his hoof in them?

Do you also know about Philippe's brother, who was scratched by a cat? **He's called Claude!**

Which reindeer keeps creeping up the wall?

Ivy!

Which reindeer wants pants for Christmas?

Nicholas!

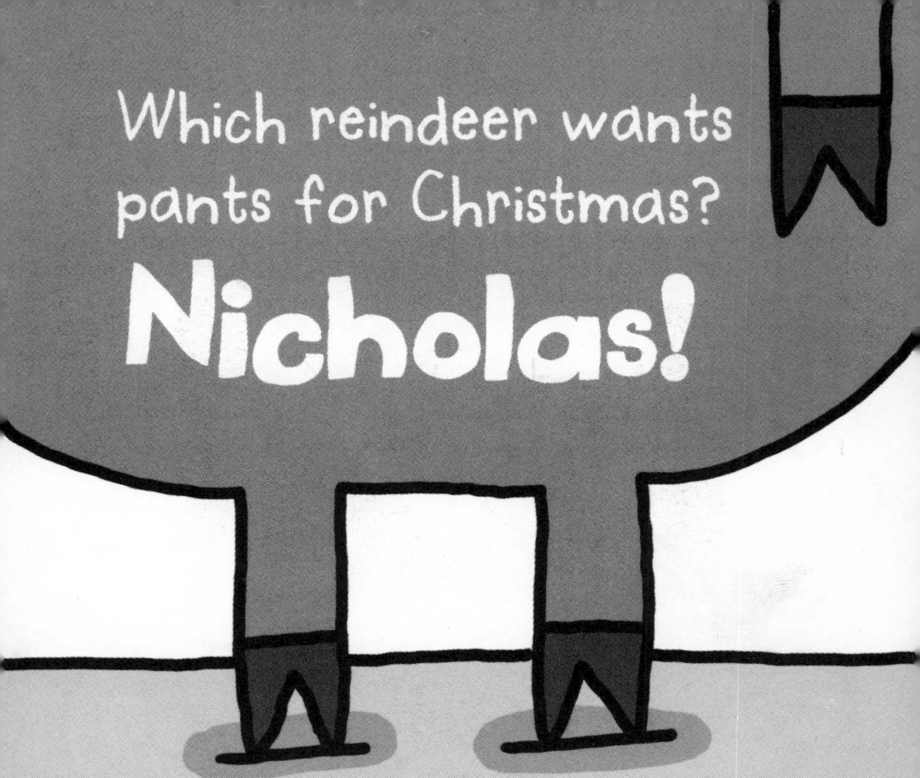

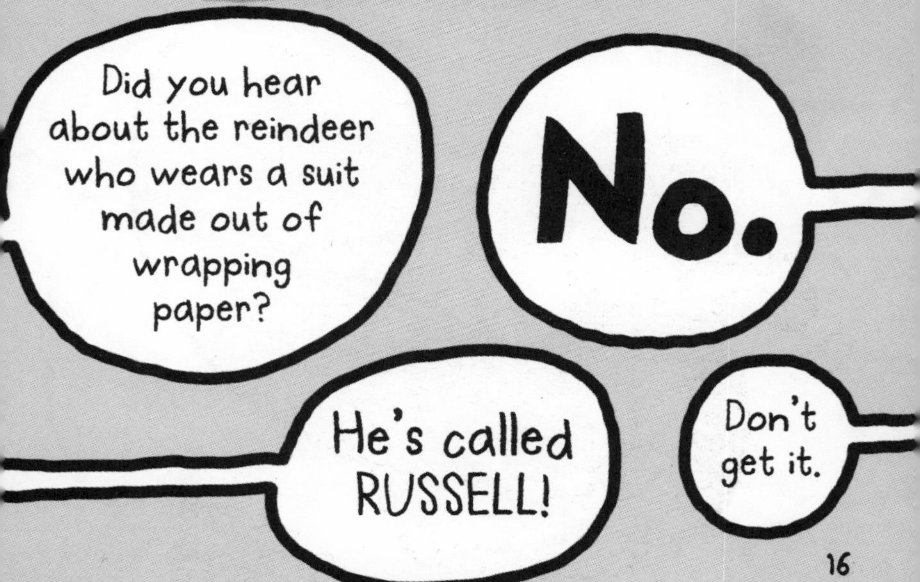

What do you call the two reindeer who stand side by side and navigate the sleigh?

Tom Tom!

19

Which reindeer stands between two goalposts while the other reindeer kick footballs at her?

Annette!

Which reindeer is always exercising?

Jim!

What reindeer has a shovel sticking out of his head?

Doug!

What reindeer DOESN'T have a shovel sticking out of his head?

Douglas!

Have you met the really funny duck who tells Christmas jokes?

beak looks like my nose!

He's a Christmas quacker!

Can I just say, this is not a reindeer joke either.

Knock knock knock jokes!

Everyone loves knock knock jokes, so here are about twelve billion of them...

These are bogies inside a nostril
tube, in case you didn't know.

Knock knock!

Who's there?

The interrupting bum

The interrupting bum wh–

PARP!

Knock knock
Who's there?
Owls go twit.
Owls go twit who?
Yes they do!

owl

cross
mouse

Knock knock!

Who's there?

A big puh

A big puh who?

Yuk!

Knock knock!

Who's there?

Europe

Europe who?

No, YOU'RE a poo!

Hi!

Knock knock!
Who's there?
Knock knock!
Knock knock who?
Knock knock!
Who's there?
Knock knock!
Knock knock who?
Knock knock!
WHO'S THERE?!
The annoying woodpecker!
The annoying woodpecker who?
Knock
knock
knock
knock
knock!

Knock knock

Who's there?

Mary

Mary who?

Mary Christmas!

Groan

32

Knock knock

Who's there?

Turkey

Turkey who?

Turkey's broken. Can you let me in?

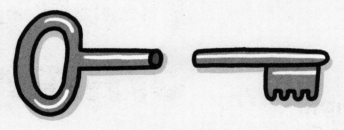

Double groan

Knock knock

Who's there?

Mary

Ooh, let me guess, Mary Christmas?

Mary Smith.

Triple groan

Knock knock
Who's there?
A pile up
A pile up who?
Eww,
GROSS!

pile of poo,
get it?

Knock knock!
Who's there?
Olaf.
Olaf who?
That's very nice, but I
only like you as a friend...

chuckling at
own joke

Knock knock

Who's there?

Theodore

Theodore who?

Theodore handle fell off,
can you let me in please?

Knock knock
Who's there?
Orange
Orange who?
Orange you going to let me in?

Knock knock
Who's there?
Doris
Doris who?
Doris locked, can you open it?

I'm really enjoying all these door jokes!

Knock knock

Who's there?

Don

Don who?

Don know where my keys are. Can you let me in?

me again, just wanted to repeat how much I like door jokes!

40

Knock knock

Who's there?

Annie

Annie who?

Annie da wee!

nnnnng!

Knock knock
Who's there?
Wayne
Wayne who?
Wayne da Manger!

Knock knock

Who's there?

Anna

Anna who?

Anna partridge in a pear tree!

actual photo of partridge →

Knock knock
Who's there?
Who
Who who?
Who who!

Who
who who
who?

I'm sorry, you've failed
your Santa audition.
Please try again next year!

Christmas pressies

The best part of Christmas day is opening all your presents! After that, all that's left to do is read some jokes about them...

I'm the ghost of Christmas present!

What's the best Christmas pressie in the world?

A broken drum – you can't beat it!

46

My granny got me a book
on anti-gravity for Christmas.

It's comperleeterly
impossible to put down.

For Christmas my other
granny got me a broken
pencil.

What a pointless pressie!

My uncle gave me a bit of old rope for Christmas. Did I like it?

I'm a frayed knot!

Guess what my mum got me for Christmas. Three holes filled with water.

Well well well.

I know you probably don't want to hear about ALL my Christmas pressies, but this year my auntie got me one glove. On one hand it fitted really well. On the other...

Who do crabs send their Christmas lists to?

Sandy Claws!

You know how you're comperleeterly over hearing about my Christmas pressies? Well, for Christmas my baby brother Des got me an empty box. He said it was nothing.

Barry

P.S. I know Des can't really speak.

What should you give a vampire for Christmas when he's feeling a bit ill?

Coffin medicine!

hates saying thank you

Why does it take Santa eight billion hours to deliver all the pressies to the centipede's house?

So.
Many.
Stockings.

Who do cats send their Christmas lists to?

Santa Claws!

Just loads of wrapping paper please

What Christmas pressie do you give a bird you don't really like?

Something cheep!

Who do cans of fizzy orange send their Christmas lists to?

Fanta Claus!

School jokes!

School is rubbish. But jokes about it are keeeeeeeel!

Which teacher tries to kiss the other teachers at Christmas?

Miss L. Toe!

What was Santa's favourite subject at school?

Xmaths!

What do Santa's elves learn at school?

The elfabet!

Which Christmas play keeps getting interrupted by purring?

The cat-ivity play!

PURRR

Why should you bring spiky leaves into school when you break up for Christmas?

Because it's the hollydays!

Which Christmas play is acted out completely upside down?

The bativity play!

Which teacher is always late to the Christmas party?

Miss D. Bus

66

Which Christmas play is just people wiping their feet all the way through?

The door-mativity play!

Which teacher doesn't understand the true meaning of Christmas?

Mister Point

Which Christmas play is hard to watch because all the characters are too small to see?

The gnat-ivity play!

shepherd gnat

Which Christmas play is hard to watch because all the characters are too small to see AND it makes your head itch?

The NIT-ivity play!

What is it like when it
snows in the playground?

It's cool!

Christmas food!

Mmm, I love Christmas lunch! Specially when someone tells a joke in the middle of it and I snort a Brussels sprout out my nose.

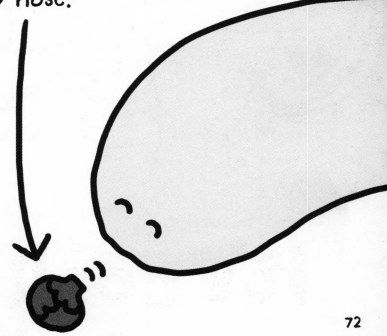

Which Christmas treats are really nosey?

Mince spies!

Which Christmas dessert is really greedy?

The Yule hog!

What's the easiest Christmas dessert to make?

A mere trifle!

Which Christmas food was born in a stable in Bethlehem?

The little baby cheeses!

What does Dracula pour
on his Christmas turkey?

Grave-y!

What is the best
Christmas pizza?

Deep-pan, crisp and even!

Two clocks were eating Christmas dinner. One was still hungry, so he went back four seconds.

TICK TOCK!

Which Christmas veggie is always down the gym?

The muscle sprout!

Doctor Doctor, I've got Brussels sprouts in my hair, in my armpits and in my pants!

You need to start eating more sensibly!

What do you call a piece of spaghetti trying to sneak into Christmas dinner?

An impasta!

What do Santa's elves make their sandwiches with?

Shortbread!

normal
size

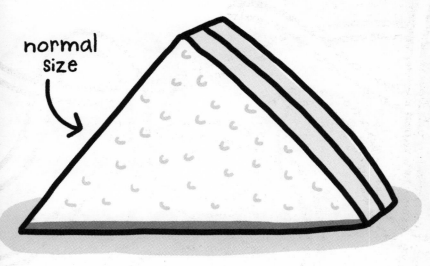

elf
size

Which Christmas treats are very dishonest?

Mince lies!

does being eaten hurt?

no!

Who likes eating Chinese food for Christmas dinner?

Noodolph!

Which Christmas treats have eight legs and eat flies?

Mince spiders!

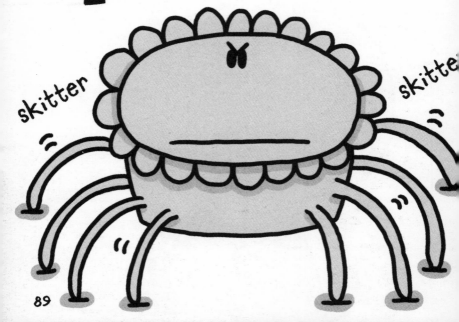

What winter holiday do potatoes celebrate?
Crispmas!

What doesn't Dracula like for his Christmas dinner?

Steak!

*fake stake

Party time!

My mum and dad have a Christmas party every year. The weird thing is, they have it in August. Only joking! Here are some slighterly better Christmas party jokes...

Which animal should you avoid at the Christmas party? **The mistletoad!**

hello there!

Who spends the Christmas party making jokes?

Banta Claus! HEE! HA! HO!

Why couldn't the skeleton go to the Christmas party?

He had no body to go with!

I'll just watch Netflix instead

A bear walked into Santa's Christmas party.
'I'd like a . . . . . . mince pie please,' he said.
'Why the big pause?' asked Santa.
'I've had these all my life!' said the bear.

What do Mr and Mrs Ghost serve at their Christmas parties?
Ice Scream!

waaah!

Why are Mr and Mrs Centipede always late to the Christmas party?

They take ages to get their boots on!

Why did the snowman cause a stir at the Christmas party?

He was naked apart from a scarf!

brrrrr!

My granny's Christmas
party trick is to eat a clock.

It's time-consuming!

hello, tick,
dear, tick!

My uncle's Christmas party trick is to crush a can of Fronkle with his bare hands.

It's soda pressing!

not funny

For our Christmas party my mum made some cardboard pressies that explode when you pull them apart.

They were crackers!

My little brother's Christmas party trick is to come down the chimney and land in the fireplace.

It's grate!

Future Ratboy's Christmas party trick is to make his whole left side disappear.

It's all right!

Future Ratboy's other party trick is to hide in the bin.

It's
rubbish!

My mum's Christmas party trick is to count to 100, missing out all the even numbers.

It's odd.

really bored

99 97 "9

95 93

89

87 " "8

Christmas songs!

There's nothing like standing round the piano with your whole family, singing Christmas songs. It's especially nothingy round my house, because we haven't got a piano.

What does one elf sing to another elf who he really likes?

Freeze a jolly good fellow!

Which Christmas carol should you sing in the desert?

Oh camel ye faithful!

What's a dog's favourite Christmas carol?

Bark, the herald angels sing!

SNOW JOKE!

How exciting is it when it snows? Even more exciting than when you're about to read some snow jokes!

How did the snowman get fit?
He rode an icicle!

Have you seen that huge abominable snowman that is crashing around outside?

Not yeti!

Me and my friend Bunky
were so excited to go sledging.

Things went downhill fast!

I was
wondering
why the snowball
was getting bigger.

Then it hit me!

I couldn't remember why I thought making a snow boomerang was a good idea.

Then it came back to me.

What should you put on a snowman's head?
An ice cap!

What did the snowman's mum say when she saw him looking at carrots in the supermarket?

Stop picking your nose!

What is the atmosphere like between two snowmen who don't like each other?

Frosty!

What is a snowman's favourite food?
Ice-bergers

What did Mum say when Dad showed her the frost outside?

I-cy!

Why did the snowman have a turnip for a nose every year?

I don't know, he just kept picking it!

Why do snowmen have more friends than the elves?

They're cooler!

Where do snowmen do their poos?

The ig-loo!

stinks

What was it like skating on the melting ice?
It was cracking!

CREEEAK!

What goes black white black?
A penguin doing a forward roll!

What goes black white black and then does a little bow?

A penguin doing a really good forward roll!

What did the police officer shout when she caught the snowman burglar?

FREEZE!

Did you SNOW?

Here are some fascinating festive facts!

In Victorian times, mince pies were made with actual beef!

probably didn't have cow leg sticking out of it

The world's tallest snowwoman was built in 2008 in Bethel, Maine, USA. She was 37.21 metres tall, had a 6 metre long nose, and her eyelashes were made from skis.

COOEE!

In Icelandic folklore they don't just have one Santa, they have a gang of Santas called the Yule Lads who have names like Spoon Licker, Doorway Sniffer, Sausage Swiper and Meat Hook.

The idea of dragging a tree inside your house and decorating it was brought to Britain by Queen Victoria's husband, Prince Albert, who came from Germany where Christmas trees were a tradition. After dragging a tree all the way from Germany to England Prince Albert was really tired, so he invented Christmas naps.

Christmas crackers were invented in 1848 by a sweetmaker called Tom Smith*, who based the design on sweet wrappers and filled the crackers full of sweets.

Later someone said, 'Wouldn't it be keel if you put a paper hat in there that people had to wear for the whole of Christmas day?' And everyone said, 'Not really, we'd prefer the sweets.' But the first person didn't listen and put the hats in anyway.

*Jim Smith's identical twin brother.

125

The origin of Santa Claus is a Christian bishop, St Nicholas, who lived in Turkey in 4AD. He was known for being generous and giving presents to people.

One Xmas he wanted to give a bag of gold to one family and dropped it down their chimney, where it fell into a sock drying by the fire, and stockings were born!

Astronomers have had lots of different ideas about the star that the three wise men followed, including that is was a comet, a planetary alignment, or a supernova.

three
wise
noses

Santa's magic slide

Barry, Nancy and Bunky went on a trip to Lapland. They met all the reindeer and were shown round the elves' workshop and it was comperleeterly keel. Then Santa said, 'Hey guys, do you want to have a go on my magic slide?'

Barry, Nancy and Bunky said, 'Hmm, let us think about it for a millisecond . . .

YES PLEASE!'

'Keel,' said Santa, and he took them to the slide. 'Now, there's something I need to tell you about the slide, and it's very important that you listen carefully.'

Barry and Nancy listened carefully, and Bunky stared out of the window at a funny-looking bird.

'When you slide down the slide,' said Santa, 'you must yell out whatever it is that you wish for the most, and then when you get to the bottom you will land in a big pile of it.'

Barry went first. He slid down the slide and yelled,

'LOADS OF SWEETS!'

He got to the bottom of the slide and landed in a big pile of sweets.

Nancy went next. She slid down the slide and yelled,

'BOOKS!'

Nancy got to the bottom of the slide and landed in a big pile of books.

And that's how you end a Christmas joke book - with somebody landing in a big pool of wee. Have a keel rest of Christmas, loseroids!

The end!

Check out all my amazekeel other books...

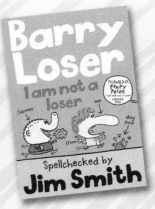

Spellchecked by
Jim Smith

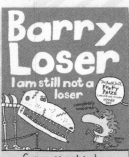

Commas put in by
Jim Smith

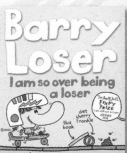

Noses drawn by
Jim Smith

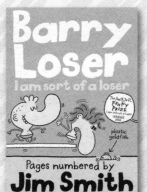

Pages numbered by
Jim Smith

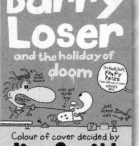

Colour of cover decided by
Jim Smith

Produced and directed by
Jim Smith

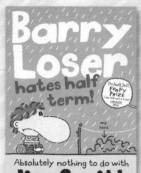

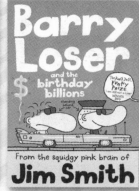

About the author and drawer

Jim Smith is the keelest kids' book author and drawer in the whole wide world amen.

He graduated from art school with first-class honours (the best you can get) and went on to create the branding for a keel little chain of coffee shops.

Jim is one of those people who gets nervous when somebody's telling him a joke in case he doesn't get the punchline.

That's why he always runs off halfway through.

and then he said . . .